Eye of The Storm
By
Mary Alford

Published by Forget Me Not Romances, a division of Winged Publications

ISBN-13: 9781980627197

Dedication:

To my sweet dog, Callie, who passed away in February 2018. Fourteen years wasn't long enough. I miss you a bunch, sweet girl, but I know you are happy and frolicking in heaven.

Scripture:

I would hasten my escape from the windy storm and tempest. Psalm 55:8

Forward:

Dear Reader,

Each of us face our own tempests in life. Finding calm can seem like an impossible wish when the storm is raging around us.

Former CIA Agent Kate Reagan finds herself in the middle of storm that has disrupted her life for six years. When Kate's entire team was killed by the terrorist they'd been chasing for months, Kate finds the only way to save her life is to pretend to lose it.

After moving dozens of times through the years, Kate ends up in the small mountain town of Soaring Eagle, Wyoming where everything about the place screams of the home she's been longing for.

Running into Deputy Sheriff Brady Connors, Kate finds herself attracted to the handsome frontier lawman right away, but having a future is not possible while the enemy is still stalking her.

With Brady's help, Kate is about face the

showdown she's been expecting for a long time, when the enemy coming after her proves to be closer than Kate could ever imagine.

I hope you enjoy Kate and Brady's story, and if you are facing your own storm right now, perhaps Kate's courage will help you get through it.

All the best…

Mary

Chapter One

Deputy Sheriff Brady Connors braked hard to keep from hitting the dog that bounded out onto the deserted stretch of county road between Alpine Glow and Soaring Eagle, Wyoming, the county seat located near Durante Mountain.

The snow continued to fall most of the day. October in Wyoming meant darkness came early. It was the darkness and deteriorating weather conditions that almost prevented Brady from seeing the dog in time.

His patrol SUV stopped a mere foot from the dog, some sort of Boxer, possibly Rhodesian-Ridgeback mix. The mutt was frozen in the same spot, blinded by the headlights.

He stared at the dog, and then scanned the area. Where had the animal come from?

Grabbing his flashlight, Brady exited the vehicle and slowly eased toward the frightened dog. "Easy there, girl," he murmured as he neared. The animal was shaking, cold, and damp from the fallen snow. Brady reached down and patted the dog's head.

From the headlight beam, he could see she wasn't injured. Definitely well taken care of. She wore a bright red collar. Brady took out his flashlight and read the dog's name. Callie. Tag had no address.

"Come on, girl. Let's see if we can find your owner." Brady gently lifted the dog up in his arms and carried her, shivering and unresisting, to the SUV.

Opening the back hatch, he set the dog inside, then closed the door. This stretch of road was remote. Only three houses near here. Brady knew two of the owners. The third place was still vacant as far as he knew.

He climbed inside the patrol vehicle and headed down the closest entrance, an overgrown drive leading to the vacant house.

It had been one bugger of a day. He'd been in court most of it, waiting to testify in the burglary case he'd worked the year before, then dealing with the defense attorney's grueling questions. All Brady wanted to do was get back to his ranch outside of Soaring Eagle and veg until morning.

Tire tracks caught his attention. Someone had been up the drive recently because the track still showed through the new-fallen snow.

Something about the circumstances felt off. Was he driving into danger? He called dispatch.

"What's up, hot shot," Jenny, the sixty-something dispatcher-slash-office manager asked in her usual straight-to-the-point manner.

"Jenny, do you know if anyone's bought the

old Pearson's place recently?"

Jenny obviously thought the question strange from the amount of time it took for her to answer. "Not that I'm aware of. Why do you ask?"

"No reason. I noticed car tracks in the drive."

"What are you doing on the driveway anyway?" An obvious question.

If he wanted to get off the radio anytime soon, he'd have to put an end to Jenny's questions. "Never mind. I'll let you know tomorrow. Goodnight, Jenny."

As Brady rounded the final curve, the answer was clear. The two-story log house was lit up like a Christmas tree.

He stopped the vehicle in front of the house and climbed out. A pickup truck was parked near the garage.

Carrying the dog in his arms once more, Brady mounted the steps and knocked on the door. He set the dog down and waited for an answer. Rustling came from inside, then the door slowly opened. The woman who greeted him was unexpected. She was dressed in jeans and a thick green sweater that matched her eyes. A few inches shorter than him, her raven-black hair cascaded over her shoulders down to her waist. She appeared a little past slender, almost as if she'd been ill and was still recovering.

Her attention riveted to the six-point gold deputy's badge pinned on his khaki shirt. That she was nervous was as easy to read as the hand that held a weapon behind her back.

"Put the weapon down, ma'am." Brady ordered

while his hand went to his holster and clutched the Glock resting in it.

She quickly complied and dropped the weapon on the table near the door. "I'm sorry. I didn't know who you were, Deputy."

That she was scared of something was easy to see. Why else would she meet him at the door with a weapon?

"You have a permit for that?" he asked casually, his gaze flicking over her face.

"I do. Would you like to see it?"

He nodded and took off his Stetson. She opened the door wide enough for him to enter. The dog ran past him. The woman spotted her for the first time. "Callie, where have you been?" She knelt in front of the dog and stroked her coat.

"I found her on the county road. She ran out in front of me. I figured she belonged to one of the houses in the area."

The woman stood. "Thank you for bringing her home. I'm still moving in, and I guess I didn't realize she'd gotten out. I'll just get that permit now." She went to her purse on the kitchen table and took something out before returning to where Brady stood near the door.

"Here you go." She handed it to him.

Brady examined the permit. It was legit. Still, he couldn't let go of the idea that something was wrong. "Any reason you need this, Ms. Reagan?" He tapped the permit.

She fidgeted and appeared to be scrambling for an answer. "Just my personal protection. I'm new to Soaring Eagle."

She was lying. "How long you been in town?" he asked. He hadn't seen her on any of his patrols, and Jenny didn't know about the sale. Jenny knew everything.

That nervous look returned to her face. She scraped back a strand of hair. It was then that he noticed the scar that ran across the left side of her face.

"A couple of days. I bought the place from Soaring Eagle Reality."

Brady found himself getting lost in the bottomless despair in her eyes. Something had happened to her.

"Thank you again for bringing Callie home. I'll keep a closer eye on her from here on out. She's my best friend, and I'd hate for something to happen to her." Kate Reagan quickly covered the scar from his view.

"No problem. I live not too far from here. I was on my way home when I spotted her." He took out his business card and handed it to Kate. "If you need anything, give me a call. My cell phone number's there and you can reach me anytime."

Her eyes widened, then she said, "I will. Thanks. This is very kind of you.

Brady sensed she was ready for him to leave, and so he headed for the door. "If you're looking for a weapon for protection, I'd recommend something with a bit more firepower. That Glock won't likely take down a bear or any other predator you'll find in this area."

He opened the door and turned to face her once more. Donning his Stetson, he tipped it her way.

"Have a good evening, Ms. Reagan."

She held the door open for him. "It's Kate, and I'll keep what you said in mind." A smiled lifted the corners of her mouth and it was his turn to freeze. She was beautiful, but haunted by something, and he wanted to know what she was running from.

~

Kate's hands shook as she shut the door and leaned against it. Her heart threatened to explode in her chest.

Six years. She'd been gone from the spy game for almost six years, and yet she hadn't been able to put the past behind her. Couldn't let her guard down with good reason. Even here, they'd keep coming after her. It was only a matter of time.

The move to Soaring Eagle was her tenth in the six-year span. She'd changed her name just as many times.

Callie sat down in front of her, peering at her with knowing eyes. Kate shoved aside the things she'd done in the name of justice. She'd learned to live in the moment.

"Are you hungry?" she asked the dog who wagged her tail. Kate dug out the dog food from the chaos in the kitchen and poured it into Callie's bowl, recalling the conversation with the deputy. Tall and handsome, he looked the part of a Sheriff's deputy, right down to his piercing blue eyes. His instincts sharp, he'd guessed right away that she was armed. He'd seen the scar too. Knew there was more to her story.

Before the last move, her former commander, Agent Jon Adler said the threat had found her in the small town in Nebraska where she was living. Kate grabbed whatever she could throw into a bag and she and Callie ran for their lives once more.

Kate was grateful that she had Jon on her side. He'd gotten her a new identity and told her to let him know when she was settled again, yet each new move took a little more out of her. She'd always known at some point there would be no more moves. It would be time to stand her ground, no matter the outcome.

Outside, an out-of-place noise captured her attention. She hurried for the Glock and slipped out the door. When the sound repeated, she kept herself close to the edge of the house and followed the noise. Drawing in a breath, she jumped around the corner of the house and flashed the light. Three raccoons were busily digging through her garbage can.

Despite the relief she felt, her legs turned to jelly. She leaned over, gripping her knees while inhaling several lungful's of crisp night air.

"Enjoy your meal, guys," she told the raccoons, and then went back inside where Callie watched the door, the hackles along her back standing at attention.

Kate relocked the door and tried to relax. She'd taken all the precautions not to leave a trail behind. Once she was positive this would be her next home, she'd called the secure number to reach her former commander. Jon was the only one who knew she was still alive. The unnerving part was the call went straight to voice mail. Almost a week had passed and there had been no word from Jon.

Fishing out the disposable cell phone from her purse, she tried the number again with the same results. Her misgivings skyrocketed.

With sleep an impossible wish, Kate closed all the curtains and checked the locks on both the doors and windows. She made coffee, then retrieved the scant amount of evidence she'd collected in the hopes of bringing down the people responsible for taking her partner's life and forcing her to have to fake her death to stay alive.

At the time, she and her team had been working hard to bring down an elusive dealer responsible for putting weapons into the hands of some of the most dangerous groups around. If her team could bring the man responsible down, it would go a long way toward putting some dangerous people behind bars. The team had tracked the man across most of Europe, then his trail went cold. A few months later, he turned up in the US.

With the help of the kingpin's trusted asset, her partner Tony had tracked down what was believed to be the man's location to an abandoned warehouse outside of D.C. The team raided it, but it had all been a setup. They were ambushed. Tony and six other team members were killed instantly. Kate was the only agent who escaped from the building with her life.

While Tony hadn't disclosed the identity of his asset, Kate believed she'd seen the woman once by accident, and there was a picture of a woman matching her description among some of Tony's notes. If she could locate the woman, perhaps she could bring Tony's killer to justice.

Kate tossed the folder she'd been reading aside. Like the countless times she'd searched the file, no answers were forthcoming. Still, she owed it to Tony and the rest of her team to find out what happened that night six years earlier. She lived while they died. The survivor's guilt was hard to overcome most days. So many times, she'd asked God why her. Why was she the one to live when so many good men had to die? Men with families who mourned them every day. So far, God was silent with His answers. Whatever the reason, she had to stay alive to find the answers she so desperately needed.

Chapter Two

Brady spotted her coming out of the grocery store and whipped the SUV over to the one vacant spot along the street, across from Mraz's Grocery. He hadn't seen her since the night they met, and yet she was always in his thoughts. He told himself it was just because of the haunted look in her eyes. The fact that she was beautiful didn't hurt any though.

He waited for Harvey Wilcox to drive by, waved, and then crossed the road to her truck.

"Need some help with those, ma'am?" he asked, his sudden appearance made her whirl around, almost dropping her bags.

"Whoa there." He grabbed two of them. "Sorry, I didn't mean to startle you." That she seemed to be hot wired for expecting trouble was another giveaway that she was running from something.

"No, that's okay," she said with a nervous lilt to her tone. She placed the third bag in the backseat of the truck. "I guess I was in my own world...I wasn't expecting you."

Her nervous response left him with the

impression that she was expecting someone. He chose to leave that discussion for another time.

"So what are you doing today besides shopping for groceries?" he asked, hoping to prolong the visit.

Her gaze narrowed, as if she were analyzing each of his words for a hidden agenda before she answered. "You're looking at it. This is my big-time Saturday experience." She smiled. It took away some of the drawn look from her face. The wind wiped her raven hair away from her cheek, revealing the scar. She was quick to cover it.

"Well, if you don't have anything perishable in those bags, I could show you around the town a little. I'm off in..." he glanced at his watch. "Now."

Immediately, the wall went up, and he wondered if she would refuse outright. A myriad of emotions crossed her face—suspicion, uncertainty, even wistfulness.

"We could grab some dinner afterwards, if you want to. Brannon's Steakhouse serves a mean ribeye." The words were out before he could stop them. Where had that come from?

He was happy that she appeared to consider it for a second before rejecting the idea. "I couldn't leave Callie alone for that long. She's been my best friend for many years." Regret slipped into the pit of his stomach, her answer not unexpected. "But I wouldn't mind taking a walk around town," she added as if she'd seen his reaction.

Brady's spirits lifted. "You wouldn't? Great. There are quite a few historic places around town." He tried to rein in his excitement. It was foolish feeling this way. He hardly knew her.

She smiled at his reaction. "I would love to see them. I'm a bit of a history buff myself."

"Well, good." He waited while she shoved something underneath the driver's seat. There was no doubt in his mind that it was the Glock he'd seen her with before.

Kate locked the door and faced him again. "I'm ready if you are."

He stared at her, amazed at how fragile she appeared, almost as if a strong wind would blow her away, yet he didn't doubt for a minute she could hold her own against any danger coming her way.

Brady pointed up ahead. "The courthouse is down here."

She walked beside him without speaking, and he wondered if he'd been misguided in asking her to take a look at the town he was so proud of. She was shivering even though it wasn't that cold out.

He pointed at the coffee shop close by. "Care for something to warm you up?" he asked and she smiled in agreement.

Brady held the door open for her and they went inside. The afternoon had left the place mostly empty. He knew the owners of the shop well enough. They'd opened the place up a few years back.

"Fred, how ya doing this afternoon?" he asked the young man behind the counter. He and his wife moved to Soaring Eagle from Billings.

"Pretty good, deputy. I guess the cold is keeping people inside today. What can I get for you two?"

Brady ordered two coffees to go and thanked the man once they had their orders.

Outside, Kate sipped her coffee as they walked. At least, her shivering stopped.

They slowed down next to the courthouse, and he showed her the historical sign near the door.

"The courthouse has been here since 1832. That's a few years after the town was formed. They used to hold hangings right over there at the gallows." He led her around to the side of the building where the old gallows still stood as a tourist attraction.

"How many people were hanged here?"

While she approached the gallows to examine it, Brady couldn't take his eyes off her. Everything about her was attractive to him, including the secrets she held inside.

She turned back, expecting an answer, and caught him watching her.

Brady cleared his throat, a little embarrassed that she'd seen him checking her out. "The records show twenty men were hanged here. Most were hardened criminals. A few cattle rustlers lost their lives as well."

Kate's eyes widened in shock. "They actually killed people for stealing cows?"

He chuckled at her surprise. "They did. In some cases, you stood a better chance of being hanged for stealing cattle than you did for taking someone's wife."

Her brow scrunched together.

"It's true. Cross my heart." He gestured and smiled.

"That must have been a hard time to live. I'm not sure I would have survived back then."

Brady didn't believe it for a minute. Underneath her fragile appearance beat the heart of a tiger. "Oh, I don't know. I think you can hold your own, and I bet you're pretty good with that Glock."

It was the wrong thing to say. The guarded look returned to her eyes. She glanced at her watch. "I should be getting back. Callie becomes anxious if I'm gone too long."

He accepted her answer with a nod, while he beat himself up on the inside for saying too much. "No problem. Why don't I just point out the rest of the interesting things as we head back to your truck?"

They started walking again. "Here's the sheriff's station where I work. It's been around a little bit longer than the courthouse." She glanced up at it.

"I love the architecture of these old buildings. You don't see anything like them today." She peered at him. "How many people work at your station?"

Her question surprised him, but he was glad she was interested. "Besides me, four people including Jenny, the dispatcher."

Kate stared at him for a few moment before speaking. Then she said, "It must be nice working in such a close-knit environment. Have you lived in Soaring Eagle all your life?"

They were almost to her truck and he slowed his steps. "I have. I grew up here. My family has lived in Soaring Eagle for over a hundred years."

"That's amazing. It must be nice to call one place your home for so long."

Ah, there it was. She traveled light with only a few possessions, and the house was sold with all the old Pearson's furnishings.

When they reached her truck, she turned to him. "Well, thank you for the tour. It was interesting." She handed him her coffee cup. "And thanks for the coffee."

Brady wasn't sure if interesting was a good thing or not. He tipped his Stetson. "You're welcome." He'd enjoyed spending time with her and hated to let her go, but he sensed she was anxious to leave.

"Maybe I'll see you around town sometime." He started to leave when her next words stopped him.

"Deputy, wait." He spun back to her, waiting. "I bought a couple of elk steaks at the store. If you wanted to drop by, say around seven, I could throw them on the grill?"

Brady drew in a breath and managed to form words. "I'd like that. See you then, ma'am." With another tip of his hat, he headed away before she had the chance to change her mind because he believed once she thought about it long enough, she would.

Once he reached his SUV, he opened the door and glanced her way. She was still standing by the truck, watching him. Keeping his hand out of sight, he slipped her coffee cup into an evidence bag. He'd have the lab run her fingerprints because that look of trepidation had returned to her face and he had to know what secrets were haunting her.

~

Kate still couldn't believe she'd invited the deputy to dinner. She couldn't afford to be forming friendships. The reality was—at a moment's notice, she'd have to leave. It was inevitable.

More surprising was that she'd enjoyed the afternoon with Brady. He was kind and sweet, and he had the most breathtaking smile. It lit up his face and held a hint of mischief that made her wonder if he was a part-time bad boy. In many ways, he reminded her of Tony. Tony had that same smile that could melt her. She'd lost her heart to him, their time together too short. Tony deserved to live beyond thirty-two.

Headlights flashing across the great room window forced her to push aside the sadness of the past. Brady was here. She glanced at herself in the hall mirror. The results of living on the run had taken its toll. Her face looked drawn, her eyes huge. She'd lost weight. The scar on her face was a constant reminder of what she'd survived.

Brady knocked, and she arranged her hair to cover the scar as best she could before answering the door.

He'd removed his hat, his dark blond hair not quite reaching the collar of his deep blue pullover sweater. The color a perfect match for his eyes.

"Hi there," he murmured with the bad-boy smile on his face, and her pulse rate kicked into overdrive.

Kate did her best to slow down her reaction. She wasn't some teenager, for crying out loud.

"Hi yourself. Come in." She stepped aside for him to enter and closed the door. He dominated the small foyer.

"How are you?" he asked. Before she could answer, Callie bounded toward him and sniffed his leg. Satisfied he wasn't a threat, the dog sat at his feet expecting to be petted.

"I'm well," she said and pointed to the dog. "I think she approves of you."

Brady bent and patted the dog's head. "She knows a dog lover, I guess. I have three of my own." Another quick smile warned her of trouble ahead for her heart, and she stepped back, putting much-needed space between them.

His jaw tightened at her reaction, but he asked, "What smells so good?"

Kate was grateful that he didn't press for answers. "Scalloped potatoes. I made a green salad as well." She gulped in a breath. "I wasn't quite sure how you liked your steak." Truth be told, she'd never prepared elk steak before.

He followed her into the kitchen. "Have you had elk before?" he asked.

"No, and I have no idea how to prepare the steaks," she said with honesty, and he chuckled.

"It takes a little finesse. They're leaner than regular steaks. How about I handle the steaks since you've made everything else."

She was grateful. "That would be nice."

He squeezed her shoulder and she tried not to pull away. She hadn't allowed herself any human contact in years. Not since Tony. Being on the run, she couldn't bear it if she put someone else's life in jeopardy because she let down her guard.

"Point me in the direction of your seasonings." She was drawing all sorts of attention to herself by her reaction to being close to him, but she couldn't help it. She'd forgotten how to do the simple things, like making small talk.

Kate opened the cabinet closest to the oven. "Everything I have is in here."

"Great. The grill is out back?" She nodded and watched as he took out several bottles, and then went out to fire up the grill.

Left alone, Kate drew in several breaths before checking on the potatoes. They were almost done. She took out placemats and silverware and set the table. Just when she was about to remove the potatoes when her cell phone's ringtone sounded, and she whirled at the sound. No one knew the number with the exception of her former CIA commander.

With hands that shook, she picked up the phone, the number unknown.

"You need to answer that?" She hadn't realized Brady had come back inside until he spoke. Her attention riveted to him. She did, but not with him so close.

Kate shook her head. "No, it's just an old friend from work. I'll call back later."

He stepped inside and closed the door. "The grill's going. I'll get these steaks on."

The message waiting beeped. She waited until Brady was outside, and then she listened.

"It's me," she barely recognized Jon's voice. He sounded troubled. "I need you to call me back as soon as you can. It's important, Kate."

The urge to talk to Jon was great, but with Brady already suspicious, she couldn't take the risk.

Instead, she removed the potatoes from the oven and took out the salad she'd prepared along with dressing.

"Steaks are almost ready." Brady came inside and announced.

"Great. I'm starving." She hoped her uneasiness wasn't reflected in her tone because she couldn't get Jon's disturbing message out of her head.

Kate carried the potatoes to the table along with the salad and handed Brady a plate for the steaks, then she accompanied him outside.

The chill of the late fall night sent a shiver through her. Instinct had her glancing around the dark countryside, looking for unseen trouble.

"You expecting company?" Brady asked with a grin that didn't quite reach his eyes.

She met his gaze. "No, just enjoying the beauty of the night. It is breathtaking, isn't it?"

He peered deep into her eyes. "It is. And peaceful, too, usually. That's why most people come to Soaring Eagle. They expect us to keep them safe. That's my job. Keeping people safe. And I'm good at it."

Chapter Three

Their conversation was surface level. Every time he tried to ask about her past, Kate changed the subject. He'd made it a point to run her name through the police database, but there was no record of a Kate Reagan anywhere. His gut told him it was a fake.

"I have apple pie if you'd like some," she said, once the table was cleared.

Brady patted his stomach. "No thank you. I'm stuffed. The food was amazing though."

She actually laughed. "Thank you. I don't get the chance to cook much. It was nice to prepare a meal for someone other than myself."

He leaned over her shoulder and placed the potatoes on the stove. "Then we'll have to do it again, won't we? But next time, you need to come to my place. It's only fair."

Brady felt her stiffen. "Maybe." Her answers were evasive and noncommittal.

He took the cup of coffee she offered and ambled to the great room where she'd made a fire.

Brady waited until she'd taken a seat before sitting next to her, searching for something to keep the conversation going.

"How do you like living in the Pearson's old place?" he asked as his eyes scanned the great room. He remembered being here when he was a kid. His dad and Jamison Pearson were friends, in spite of their different social status. Jamison grew up in Soaring Eagle, like his dad. They'd gone through school together. The bond they'd formed never went away.

"It's nice. I like the solitude." He glanced her way. A strange thing to say for someone so young. He gauged her to be in her early thirties.

"I remember the Pearsons from growing up. They were great people. Jamison passed away a few years back, and his wife went to live with her kids in Colorado. She agreed to sell the place. I don't think she took anything with her except her personal possessions."

Kate nodded. "I heard a lot about them from my real estate agent. She had nothing but good things to say."

He noticed the time. Almost eleven. Where had the time gone? Brady rose to his feet. "I should be going. I have the early shift in the morning."

"Oh." She sounded disappointed but stood and took his cup. "I had a nice time. I'm glad you came." Was she surprised that she'd enjoyed herself?

Kate set the cups on the kitchen table, and she followed him to the door, the dog trotting behind her.

He pivoted to face her in the entryway. "I had a nice time too. Hopefully, we can do it again soon," he said, unsure of what to do next. A handshake didn't feel appropriate. He leaned over and kissed her cheek, aware of her drawing in a sharp breath at the touch. "Have a good night, Kate."

Before she could answer, he headed down the steps to his truck with a smile of satisfaction. He climbed inside, turned the vehicle around, and waved as he left her place.

That she was one troubled soul was easy to read. What was she running from? What had caused that scar on her face?

"Help her, God. She needs You," he murmured the prayer into the cold night, his breath chilling the air around him.

Once he reached the edge of her drive, a flicker caught his attention. Was that a light in the woods across the county road?

Brady pulled the truck onto the shoulder and killed the engine. Taking his weapon, he tucked it behind his back and grabbed his jacket and flashlight, then hurried toward the spot where he'd seen the light. Had he imagined it?

He climbed to where he believed the light was. The damp earth below revealed a couple of sets of fresh footprints. Unease settled into the pit of his stomach, and he flashed the light around the area. Was it someone hunting illegally? Even in the peaceful community, there were still those who chose to break the law. It wouldn't be the first time he'd caught someone hunting out of season.

"Anyone there?" he called out. The tracks

veered off to the left, toward another small county road. Brady picked up his pace to follow them. He reached the road in time to see taillights disappearing around the bend. If they continued the way they were going, they'd end up in Alpine Glow.

Why were they out here in the middle of the night? His gut was screaming they were up to nothing good.

~

Kate waited until Brady drove away, then she grabbed her phone and called the number Jon left in his message. The call went straight to voice mail, as her others had, and unease slithered down her spine. After trying the number several more times, she gave up. She'd have to wait for him to call her back.

She carried the coffee cups to the sink and washed them out, then flipped the coffee maker off.

What had Jon discovered that made him need to talk to her so urgently? Her imagination raced over the possibilities. Was he trying to warn her that the man hunting her had found her again? The thought was crippling. The moves were coming more frequently. The enemy was getting better at tracking her.

The darkness outside made her feel exposed and vulnerable. Kate hurried to close all the curtains, her pulse racing. She rushed to the desk and took out the Glock from where she'd stored it before Brady arrived.

Despite some awkward moments, she enjoyed the evening. Every time he asked a question that was a little too personal, she had to change the subject.

Brady was a sweet guy, and handsome as all get out. She'd give anything to invite him over again, yet it was best if she kept her distance. She couldn't afford to make personal connections with anyone, and why take the chance of hurting him when she had to disappear in the middle of the night?

Kate was too restless to think about sleep. With Callie curled up in front of the fire, she took out the file folder that held information to help her track down the people trying to kill her.

As always, that night six years earlier came to mind, fresh as if it were still that time. The team had gone into the warehouse on a tip and straight into an ambush. They'd been set up and many of the agents died that night. Tony Kirk, their leader and the man she loved, among them.

Tears filled her eyes as she recalled Tony's handsome face. Brady reminded her a lot of him. Both handsome in their own way, but it was their exuberance, their playful, flirty behavior that made them both stand out.

She and Tony had just begun to date before the attack. He finally wore her down, and she agreed to go out to dinner. It wasn't long before she was in love with him. They kept their relationship secret. No one knew, with the exception of Jon.

All she had on the case was the photos and a personal notebook she'd grabbed from Tony's apartment in D.C. Kate knew him well enough to know he kept a personal file on the case. She'd found the folder. The single name of Tony's asset,

Maria, was little to go on. A phone number disconnected for six years and a photo that showed the woman from the side, taken in what looked like a park. Tony's notes were vague. Maria got in touch with him. She claimed to know the name of the weapon's dealer because she worked for him. According to Tony, she had confirmed several of the locations where the team had come close to capturing the dealer.

In the folder were several photos of the warehouse where they'd been ambushed. Not much to go on. She'd tried numerous times to track down Maria without any luck. Kate was beginning to wonder if she would ever find out the woman's real name.

She closed the folder and put it away. "I'm sorry, Tony, I'm trying. I just need a little help."

The silence of the night closed in around her and she grew restless. Making more coffee was the last thing she needed, and yet she did, because sleep wasn't possible. Every time she closed her eyes, she was back there in the warehouse. The fear on Tony's face was the first thing that got her attention. He'd turned and yelled at her to run. She headed for the entrance, certain he was right behind her. She'd almost made it when the world around her exploded and she woke up in the hospital, only to be told that she was the only survivor. Tony, her love, was gone, and from that day forward, the revenge in her heart gnawed away at her happiness. Kate was determined to do whatever it took to bring Tony's killer to justice, no matter the cost.

She touched the silver cross necklace lovingly.

Tony gave it to her shortly before the attack. It was all she had left of him.

Pouring coffee, she took it outside to make sure the grill was turned off. A light snow had begun to fall, so she stayed for a moment to enjoy the beauty. Growing up in Texas, snow was a rarity. Through her years with the CIA, she'd been to dozens of places across the world, and she'd seen some wonderful sights, but the moment she landed in Soaring Eagle, Wyoming, she knew this was the place she'd been looking for. A place to put down roots. If only that were possible.

Something caught her attention. Was that a light in the woods above the house? Fear froze her in place for a moment, then she rushed inside and locked the door.

Kate crept to the window and parted the curtains. The light disappeared. Was it real or just her imagination? Why would someone be in the woods at this time of the night? They'd found her again.

Chapter Four

In the light of day, as he drove by the spot where he'd seen the light, Brady's bad feeling refused to leave. He turned onto the county road where he'd seen the vehicle disappear. Last night's snow had partially covered the tracks. He drove a little ways down and didn't see any spot where they might have turned around.

Brady grabbed his cell phone and called his friend, Wallace Chambers, who was a game warden for the area.

"Hey buddy, how are you doing? Wallace said, recognizing the number.

"Pretty good, I guess, but I ran across a strange occurrence last night." Brady told him about the light in the woods.

"Could be illegal elk hunters. I've arrested a few of them recently. I wouldn't be surprised if there weren't more. Some people pay big money for an elk head stuffed."

The thought was repulsive. "Cowards, all of them."

"They are. Anyways, I'll take a look around the spot and let you know what I find out."

"Thanks, Wallace. I appreciate the help." Brady disconnected the call and dropped the phone in the seat beside him.

As much as he wanted to believe what happened out there was just a couple of illegal hunters, he didn't. This went much deeper.

Did it have something to do with Kate? She was definitely running from something. Had her trouble followed her to Soaring Eagle?

He drove through town and parked in front of the station. Since it was Sunday, he was the only deputy on call, and he planned to get caught up on paperwork and hopefully check in with the lab to see if they had the results from Kate's coffee cup.

Taking off his Stetson, he hung it on the coat rack, then sat down at his desk. A handful of messages awaited him. One from the lab caught his immediate attention. He'd call the others back soon. First, he wanted to talk to the lab.

"Donny, you got my results back?" Brady asked.

The length of time it took for Donny Everett to answer did little to settle Brady's unease.

"I do, but you're not going to like it. She's not a criminal. Her prints are on file with the government somehow. When I tried to search them, I got shut down. I don't know who she is, but I'm betting she's being protected for a reason."

"Geez," Brady blew out the word. "I appreciate your help, Donnie. I hope I didn't get you into trouble by looking them up."

"Naw, I'll be fine. I'll make up some excuse. Sorry I couldn't be of much help. Let me know if you need anything else."

"Will do." Brady hung up the phone and stared into space. What the heck was going on here? The only explanation he could think of was she was either a federal witness, or a federal agent. If she were in Witness Protection, their office would have been notified. Which left the other possibility—she was a spy. That explained her cagey looks, the gun that was always close by, and the feeling she moved around a lot. She was hiding out from someone bad. What trouble was she bringing to their quiet community?

Brady returned the necessary phone calls, and then cleared away some paperwork. He was almost finished with his pile when someone came into the station. He glanced up from what he was reading and saw her standing near the door. Kate.

Rising to his feet, he joined her at the door. "Hey, this is a nice surprise. What brings you to the station?" It occurred to him that maybe she hadn't come here specifically to see him. He noted the tightness framing her lips. "Is anything wrong?"

She took her time answering. "I'm not sure."

"Come have a seat," he gestured with his hand, then pulled out a chair for her. Once she'd sat, he circled his desk and did the same. "Now, tell me what's troubling you."

Kate smiled at him. "I'm probably being silly, but last night after you left, I saw a light behind my house. I had gone outside to check on the grill and saw it. By the time I went inside, it was gone. Is that a normal happening around here?"

Her words sent chills up his spine because it matched what had happened to him. "No, not usually." He didn't want to worry her unnecessarily, so he chose not to tell her about what happened to him. "Have you seen lights out there before?"

She shook her head. "No, never. This is the first time."

He asked the question he knew she wasn't going to like, but he needed answers, and she hadn't been forthcoming. "Any reason why someone would be coming after you?" He held her gaze as her lips tightened. She was obviously steeling herself from giving too much away.

"No, of course not."

Still he couldn't let it go. "No angry ex-boyfriends who can't let you go?" he half-heartedly teased. There was more to her story, and he needed her to open up to him.

Kate looked away. "There's no one."

He didn't believe her. "If it will make you feel more at ease, I could stop by after work and take a look around."

Her eyes darted up and she shook her head too quickly for his liking. "No, that's okay. I'm sure it's nothing." She got to her feet. "Thank you, Brady. I'm sorry I bothered you."

He followed her to the door. "It's no bother. That's what I'm here for. I'll stop by after my shift and check on you."

She smiled. "You don't have to do that."

Brady leaned against the doorframe and managed a grin. "I want to. I have to take care of my constituents. You never know, one day when the sheriff retires, I might just run for the office."

She burst out laughing. "Oh really? Well, I wouldn't want to stand in the way of such a lofty goal."

He chuckled at her joke. "Well then, I'll see you later."

She waved and left him standing in the doorway watching her. Why would a spy come to Soaring Eagle if she wasn't running from something dangerous?

~

"This way, Callie." Kate hiked up to the spot behind the house where she'd seen the light the previous night. Several sets of footprints remained. She followed them with Callie bounding ahead of her, happy for the outing.

It had been a foolish move to stop by the sheriff's station. Brady was already curious about her. He was a good cop. He knew something was off in her story and had probably begun to check her out already. She would, if the tables were turned.

As she continued following the footprints, Kate stopped dead, a sound capturing her attention. It sounded like running water. She hurried ahead and spotted a river, close to overflowing its banks. She couldn't believe a river was so close to her house and she didn't know it. The tracks stopped at the river's edge. Something had been stored there. She went over to the spot and knelt, studying the evidence of something heavy being dragged in the dirt. Did the men have a boat stashed here? Who were they?

She rose to her feet and scanned the area across the river. Nothing stirred there. Was she paranoid? It could be someone fishing the river. Still, the unease gnawing at her wouldn't let her accept that answer. Where was Jon? More than fourteen hours had passed since she'd received the call from him, and he still wasn't picking up. Something was wrong.

Callie sniffed around the spot where the boat had been stored, picking up the men's scent. Kate felt exposed out in the open like this. If someone were looking for her, she'd need to stay out of sight.

"Come, Callie." She pivoted on her heel and headed back toward the house at a fast pace. Kate had just topped the ridge above her place, when a branch snapping close by had her whirling toward the sound.

A man she didn't recognize stood a few feet from her. Right away, Callie's ridge stood at attention and she growled low, her stance defensive.

Kate drew the Glock and pointed it at the man. "That's far enough."

The man spotted the weapon and froze. "Whoa. Sorry, I didn't mean to startle either of you."

"What are you doing up here? This is private property."

The man continued to eye the weapon. "I didn't realize, sorry. I thought I was still on national forest property. I was out hiking, and I guess I lost my way."

Kate didn't believe his story, and she didn't like the way he stared at her as if he recognized her. "What's your name?" He didn't look like a terrorist, but then again, she had no idea what the face of the man hunting her looked like.

"Steve Ward." He held out his hand. "It's nice to meet you."

Kate didn't take his hand. "Do you live near here?"

Ward seemed to take offense at her questioning. "Now what business is that of yours?"

"It's mine because you're on my property. Now answer my question." She kept the Glock pointed at the man's chest, not trusting him for a minute.

While Ward was dressed in hiking gear, Kate was almost certain he had a gun tucked underneath his jacket.

"All right. No, I'm not from around here. I'm visiting."

He was lying. "I'm calling the sheriff's office."

Ward's eyes darted from her eyes to her gun. "Now, now, there's no need. I'm leaving. I'm sorry to have troubled you."

Before Kate could stop him, he turned and headed toward the neighboring property at a fast pace with Callie at her heels.

"No, Callie. Stay!" Kate sensed the dog's reluctance when she returned to her side. Then they spun around and ran the rest of the way back to her house.

Once inside, she locked the door, her heart pounding against her chest. There was no way Ward had just happened onto her property. The nearest national forest was a good two miles away.

She grabbed her cell phone and called Jon's number once more. Still no answer. Desperate, she needed help. Kate took out the card Brady had given her and called his cell phone.

"Deputy Connors." He answered on the first ring.

"Brady, its Kate. I just ran into a trespasser on my property." She stopped for a breath, then recounted the run-in with Ward.

"Are you safe now?" he asked.

"Yes, I'm inside the house."

"Good. Stay there. I'm on my way." He didn't wait for her response. She ended the call, relieved that someone was on her side. She was terrified that something bad had happened to Jon and it was all because of her.

Chapter Five

"Hey Frank, I just had a call from the owner of the Pearson's old place. Someone was trespassing on her property. I'm going to head over and check it out." Brady holstered his weapon and slung on his jacket.

Sheriff Frank Lawson glanced up from reading something, his glasses at the end of his nose. Frank had been the sheriff of Durante County for going on ten years and was well-respected by his constituents for being fair and approachable.

"You need backup?" Frank asked, lines forming on his forehead.

"No...at least not for the moment. I'll call you once I've assessed the situation."

Frank removed his glasses. "Be careful. I don't like the sound of this."

"I will." Brady headed for the door when Jenny popped her head into the office.

"Sarah Barnes just called. She says she has another prowler."

Brady froze, his gaze whipping to Frank's.

Sarah's place was next to Kate's. While Sarah Barnes was going on eighty years old and reported having a prowler at her place at least once a week, coupled with Kate's call, it made him uneasy.

"I'll call in Aamon to check out Sarah's complaint. You go take care of your call."

Brady charged from the station through the falling snow to his patrol vehicle. Hopping into the SUV, he hit the lights and floored the gas. It was a ten-minute drive to Kate's place, yet the late fall weather wasn't doing its part to cooperate. Several new inches of snow had hit Soaring Eagle overnight and an ugly winter storm was on its way.

With siren and lights flashing, he turned onto Kate's drive and slid his way to her house.

He hurried up the steps and Kate met him at the door.

He could tell she was upset by the encounter. "Has anything new happened?" he asked.

She shook her head. "No, nothing. I haven't seen him again. Maybe he was who he said he was."

Brady didn't believe it for a minute. "It's doubtful. We're not that close to the national forest. I'm going to check in with your neighbor, Sarah Barnes. She reported a prowler a little while ago."

A furrow formed between her eyebrows. She said, "You think it was him? He was heading in that direction."

"It's possible, but I won't know until I talk to Sarah. Another deputy's heading over to take her statement, but I'll just go speak with her first."

She followed him to the door. "Be careful. He might still be out there."

The concern in her eyes warmed his heart. "I will. Stay inside and keep the door locked."

He waited until she'd locked the door before easing toward Sarah's place. Brady had barely cleared the property line before Sarah hurried down the steps of her house to meet him.

"Thank goodness you're here, Deputy Connors. I just don't know what to make of it."

Brady put his best smile in place and tried not to alarm the woman. "Make of what, Ms. Barnes? What's going on today?"

"Over here." Unlike her normal jovial manner, Sarah Barnes was all business today.

Brady followed her to the left side of the house, closest to Kate's. She pointed at something on the ground. "You see these?"

On the ground not far from the house were multiple footsteps. Had there been more than one person out there?

Brady knelt and examined the prints. At least two different shoe types. The size had him guessing they both belonged to males.

"When did you first notice the footprints, Ms. Barnes?"

Her hands wouldn't stop fidgeting. "Right before I called Jenny. I was outside feeding the chickens when I came back this way and saw them."

The footprints were fresh all right. There was very little snow in the tracks.

"Anything broken into?" he asked.

Sarah shook her head. "Not that I can tell."

Brady stood. "Okay, do me a favor and go

inside the house and wait for me. Deputy Aamon Lone Elk is on his way over and he'll take your statement. In the meantime, I'm going to take a look around and see if I can find anything."

Sarah met his gaze. For the first time since he'd met her, she appeared frail. "Should I be worried?" she asked, a frown knitted her brows together.

"Let's not jump to conclusions yet. Let me have a look around. You stay inside until Aamon arrives."

Brady waited until the woman had gone into the house before he tracked the footsteps. They were leading toward the woods that separated Sarah Barnes' home from Kate's. One set headed up behind the house to the ridge where Kate had encountered Ward.

He didn't like it. First the lights in two separate directions the night before, and now this. The time for secrets was over. He needed Kate to tell him what she was running from.

~

Callie let out a low growl and charged for the door, pawing at it. Fear gelled in the pit of Kate's stomach as she grabbed the Glock and eased to the window. At the edge of the property, Brady was examining the ground.

Kate tucked the weapon behind her back, slipped on her coat and went outside.

The sound of the door closing must have drawn his attention from what he was doing. He watched her for a moment, then headed her way.

She continued walking toward him, all the while trying to gauge his facial reaction. Before she could voice her worst fears aloud, she knew something had happened.

"What did you find?" she asked, waiting for him to say the words aloud.

He pointed behind him. "Someone was walking around Sarah's place. There were two sets of footprints in the snow. One set appeared to stay in the woods, no doubt watching your place. The second set went up to the ridge. I'm guessing that's this Ward person you ran into earlier."

Was Ward the man chasing her? She glanced past him at the footprints in the snow. "Is she okay?"

He nodded. "Yes, she's fine. Just a little upset." He went over to the footprints and pointed to them. She followed at a distance. "Whoever was at Sarah Barnes' place came this way. Probably not more than an hour ago."

Kate studied the two separate sets of steps. "It looks as if they kept to the edge of the woods, out of sight."

He stared at her through narrowed eyes. She'd given too much away.

"That would be my assumption as well. Nice observation."

She shrugged. "A lucky guess. Do you think they're dangerous?"

Kate could tell there was more he wanted to say but kept it to himself. "I think you know the answer to that more than I do, don't you, Kate?"

She couldn't draw her gaze from his face. "I don't know what you're talking about," she murmured, knowing he didn't buy it.

"I think you do. We need to talk. But first, I'm going to wait for Aamon to show up. I'll stop back by when he's here and Sarah is safe."

He pivoted to leave before she could force words out. She should tell him there was no need; she'd be okay on her own, but the truth was, the evidence of someone so close to her house had her spooked.

With nothing left to do, Kate returned to her house and locked the door. She'd barely been here a few days. Was it possible that they'd found her so soon?

Kate tried Jon's number again, the results the same. What had happened to him? He'd always have answered her call in the past.

She dialed the number of one of her colleagues, Mark Franklin. She trusted Mark to keep the truth secret.

"Mark...its Sidney Michaels." She waited for those words to register.

"Sid...but I thought...You're supposed...You're dead," Mark blurted out in a strangled tone.

She swallowed back regret. Jon had helped her come up with that cover story. She'd faked her death in a car accident which allowed her to disappear. No one was supposed to be looking for Agent Sidney Michaels anymore. Only it hadn't worked.

"But...how?" Mark asked, struggling to accept the reality.

"It's complicated. The less you know at this point, the better. I don't have time to explain what's happened, but I need to speak with Jon right away. I've been trying to reach him on the number he gave me, only he's not answering. Have you talked to him recently?"

The silence that followed was alarming. "No. Not for a few days. He called in and said he was taking a week of vacation. Said if we needed to reach him we could leave a message and he would be in touch."

Jon taking a vacation? In all the years she'd known him, he'd never once taken even a sick day. She tried to digest this information logically but knew if Jon had gone missing, the results weren't going to be good.

"Sid, does this have something to do with what happened outside of D.C.?"

Remembering that night was hard. "I think so. You have to find him, Mark. Something's going on and I think Jon may be in danger."

"Where are you? Do you need me to bring you in?" Mark asked, his words clipped.

That was the last thing she needed. "No, and its best you don't know where I'm at, for everyone's sake. Listen, I'm going to take another crack at finding Tony's asset. If I can locate her, maybe I can figure out the name of the man responsible for this before Jon is harmed. I just need you to find him."

Mark blew out a breath. "All right. I'll call him and leave him a message, then I'll stop by his place and see if I can find anything useful. Can I call you back to let you know what I find out?"

She was quick to answer. "No, I think its best if

you don't. I'll contact you."

"Okay," he breathed the word out. "Stay safe, Sidney, and when this is all over, I want to know where you've been for the past six years."

She disconnected the call without answering, her hands trembling. Jon was missing. Her instincts were telling her Mark wouldn't be able to reach him.

Kate grabbed the notebook where Tony kept his personal thoughts on the case. She'd pored over the notes a dozen times, knowing that somewhere in there was something important.

Before she opened the book, a knock sounded on her door, so she stuffed it back into the desk drawer and closed it.

She hurried to the door and confirmed it was Brady before opening it.

"Is Sarah okay?" she asked, hating that another innocent person was involved in her problems.

"She'll be okay. She's a pretty tough lady." The grim expression on his face informed her that what she'd dreaded the most was about to happen.

He stepped inside and closed the door. "Can we sit?"

Her heart kicked up a beat. She struggled to appear normal and pointed to the great room.

Once they were seated, she waited for him to speak, her hands clenched.

"The footprints circled back around to the road. I'm guessing the ones you saw at the river were made by someone else. Maybe a trapper or someone fishing. Ward and his partner must have had a car waiting at the road." He stopped for a second.

"Here's the thing. I don't think Sarah Barnes was the person they were watching. It think it was you."

Chapter Six

Her face gave little away, but her eyes told a different story. They spoke of someone who had seen a lot of bad things in the past. His cop's instinct was telling him she was ex-military or something more covert…like a spy.

"Why would you think they were watching me?" She forced out.

She wasn't going to be forthcoming. It didn't escape his notice that wasn't in the line of sight from the windows. He could see she had the Glock tucked behind her back. If he were a betting man, he'd say she was CIA.

"Because until this time, there's never been a legitimate thing about Sarah Barnes' claims having a prowler. Then you move in and suddenly trouble arrives for real." She started to answer, but he stopped her. "Then there's the fact that you're hiding from something. I bet if I examined your credentials carefully they'd prove to be fake." He pinned her eyes. "Who are you really, Kate? Military…CIA."

The tiniest of blinks confirmed he'd landed on

the truth.

"That's ridiculous. I'm not military or CIA or anything. I just moved here because I wanted a fresh start."

He shook his head. "What are you running from, Kate or whatever your name is? Who are you working for?"

"No one," she dropped her gaze from his.

"I ran your prints from the coffee cup the other day. You're in the federal database. Maybe I should call the CIA and send them a picture of you."

She bolted to her feet. "No...Stop."

Finally, the truth. "All right, so which is it?"

Kate paced the room, her words coming in fits and starts. "I was CIA. I...left...six years ago."

Brady stared up at her. There was more to her story, he could see.

"Why'd you leave?" It was an obvious question, and yet the long pause showed how difficult it was for her to talk about.

"Because my partner and my entire team was killed in an explosion outside of D.C. I was the only one to survive." Slowly her story unfolded. Because of the dangerous people chasing her, Kate had been forced to fake her death, in hopes that the threat would go away. It hadn't. The man responsible for taking out her team was ruthless and determined to end her life before she could put him away forever.

"I barely got away the last time, but I thought I'd be safe here." Kate shook her head. "And now the only man who knows where I am is missing."

He listened while she told him about her commander's presumed vacation.

"You think they took him to get to you?" Brady asked, shocked by the admission.

He saw the truth before she nodded. "I'm worried." She went over to the desk and pulled out a file. "I've been through Tony's notes dozens of times, and I'm positive there's something in them that will help me find his asset, and yet..." She didn't finish.

"You need a fresh set of eyes," Brady announced, and she whirled to face him.

"I couldn't ask you to do that. I'm putting you and everyone else's life in danger by being here. I should go."

"You going to keep running forever? Or until you die?" Noticing her wince, he approached her at the desk. "I know I may not be CIA, but I do know law enforcement. Let me take a look at what you've got. Maybe I can see what you're too close to."

"Okay," she slowly agreed, but I'm not letting that file out of my sight. It's all I've got of...it's the only evidence I have."

Brady nodded. "No problem, but there is one thing. If this is the guys who killed your team, they know you're here. They're probably watching your place. You can't stay here."

"What do you have in mind? You want to arrest me, Deputy Connors?" She smiled, and it left him feeling a little unsettled. It had been a long time since he had a serious relationship. Mostly he played the field, but that was growing old quickly.

"Nothing like that," he told her, returning her smile. "I was going to suggest you and Callie come to my ranch and stay until this is over. We just have to get you out of here without the men noticing."

She thought about it for a moment. "Why don't I meet you in town after your shift ends?"

Brady moved to the door. "That will work. You know where the sheriff's office is?"

"I do."

"Good. I'll see you there in…" he glanced at his watch. "Five hours. In the meantime, stay out of sight and if anything comes up, call me."

She followed him to the door. "What are you going to tell your boss?" A worried frown creased her forehead.

"The truth." She started to protest, but he held up a hand. "I mean about the footprints. It'll give me a reason to drive by a few times to make sure you're okay."

She stopped next to him by the door. "That sounds nice. Thank you, Brady."

He took her hand and squeezed it. "You're welcome. Take care of yourself. These men are obviously dangerous."

"I will, and you're right."

Brady stepped out on the porch. On instinct, he stroked her cheek. "I'll see you at the station in five hours. Don't stand me up, Kate, and don't get yourself killed."

For the first time since he'd met her, she relaxed.

"I promise I'll be at the station when your shift ends."

~

She had everything packed. It was quarter to five. Time to head to the station. Brady had left

49

Deputy Aamon Lone Elk stationed at the entrance to her drive for added protection.

Kate took one final sweep of the place. Would she ever call this home again?

Please, God...

She carried her things to the truck with Callie at her heels. After tossing her bags in the bed on the truck, she held the door open for Callie to hop in. When the dog was settled, Kate got behind the wheel.

She turned to Callie. "Ready to check out Brady's ranch?" The dog barked in response.

Kate stopped next to Aamon's parked vehicle. The deputy exited his patrol vehicle and sauntered toward her.

"You on your way over to the station?" Aamon asked.

She nodded. "Yes. Thank you for keeping watch."

He lowered his head. "It's no problem, ma'am. I haven't seen anything out of the ordinary since I've been here. I'll keep an eye out around here for a while for Ms. Barnes' sake. Are you sure you're okay to drive into town?"

As grateful as she was for his consideration, it was a ten-minute drive, and she'd hate it if anything were to happen to her neighbor.

"I'll be fine."

He tapped the side of the truck, then stepped away. Kate eased the truck from the driveway onto the county road. The recent snow had been plowed away, but the roads were slick, making the drive twice as long. Brady had told her the weatherman was predicting one of the worst winter storms of the season coming later that evening, and she was grateful she wouldn't be facing it alone.

As she neared the bridge for the river that weaved behind her place, Kate slowed her speed to a crawl. In the rearview mirror she saw it. A vehicle approached at a fast rate. Her pulse leapt to her throat. With the gathering clouds, she'd switched her lights on for safe passage. There was no way the driver couldn't see her, and yet his speed accelerated.

Kate was almost to the bridge. There was no place to escape as the massive SUV slammed against her truck at full speed. The last thing she remembered was her head slamming into the steering wheel. When she came to, her truck had landed sideways in the freezing waters of the river, the swift current smashing it against the cement foundation of the bridge.

Water filled the cab at an alarming rate. She and Callie had to get out fast. She struggled to control the panic as she unbuckled her seatbelt and freed herself of its restraints. Then grabbing Callie by the collar, she pulled herself and the dog through the window that wasn't submerged and jumped into the freezing water. The dog began paddling toward the bank.

The cold water jolted her system. She felt disoriented. Staying focused was difficult. She spotted Callie on the bank, barking at something above her.

Kate caught sight of two men standing on the bridge. One of them had a gun. Before she could duck for cover, the man fired at her, striking her in the arm. The force caused her to sink under the water. Blood mingled with the murky water and floated to the surface. Kate fought to break the surface and take a breath. She couldn't tell what caused the excruciating pain—the bullet wound or the bitter cold water. Her mind was struggling to stay conscious, but was fading fast.

"Let's go. She won't survive long. Hypothermia will get her before anyone can come to her aid." She recognized the man's voice from the bridge. It was Ward's.

Two doors slammed, and then the SUV drove away. Callie waded to the edge of the water whimpering as Kate forced her injured body to swim toward the dog. She dragged herself up on the bank, her energy spent. Callie licked her face.

"Go, Callie. Go get help." Her words slurred. She was losing consciousness and she knew if she did, she would die before help arrived. The dog barked several more times, then took off.

Kate forced herself into a sitting position. Shivering as much from the cold air as from her drenched clothes, she knew she didn't have long.

Her phone was in the truck. She couldn't call anyone. The blood was streaming down her arm. She had to stem its flow before she passed out.

It took all her strength to rip a piece of her shirt off and tie it below the wound. In the distance, Callie barked. Had the dog understood when she told her to go for help?

Please, Lord.

She was shivering violently, her teeth

chattering, ice crystals forming on her clothes. She'd faced down some harrowing situations in her time with the CIA, but nothing like this. How could she save herself now?

Crystals formed from the tears in her eyes, making it hard to see. She had to keep fighting. Giving up wasn't an option.

Kate stumbled to her feet. If she stayed here, she'd be dead. The world around her spun and her stomach heaved. If she could make it back to her house, Aamon was there.

Planting one foot in front of the other took all her concentration. She managed only a couple of steps when she had to stop and gather breath.

"Keep moving. You can't stop," she murmured to herself and pushed her foot forward a few inches. "Just a couple more steps." It wasn't the truth, but it helped her stay focused.

When her foot refused to budge, she stopped, her legs threatened to give away.

"No, you can't think like that," she chided. She wasn't giving up. There was too much at risk.

Another step, followed by another, brought her to the edge of the road. Then she saw a vehicle approaching. Had Ward and his goon returned to finish the job? She needed to get out of sight. The woods were close by, but the distance seemed light-years from where she was standing. Her legs quivered and she sank down to the ground on the edge of the road.

Staring up at the falling snow, a tear slipped from her eye. Was this how it was going to end? The thought was like a knife. She didn't want to die here without knowing the answer to why? There was a future out there for her; she'd glimpsed bits of it in Brady's smile. This wasn't how her story ended.

Chapter Seven

"Brady, there's been an accident." The minute he saw Aamon's number on his phone he knew. Kate was in danger.

"Is she alive?" he asked, dreading Aamon's answer.

"Yes, but she's in bad shape. We're almost to the hospital." Silence followed, and then, "She's been shot. Someone ran her off the road and into the river near her house. She was in the river for a while."

Shot! Alarm and guilt chewed as his stomach. He thought he could keep her safe, yet he'd been wrong.

Brady raced to his SUV and headed toward the local hospital outside of town. He hit the lights and siren and flew down the road. All he could think about was regret that she hadn't insisted she go with him. He shouldn't have let her out of his sight for a second.

He spotted Aamon's patrol vehicle parked out front. Brady slid in behind it and ran inside. The gurney carrying Kate was being wheeled toward the emergency room.

The sight of her was terrifying. The blueness of her lips and hands from hypothermia. Her arm bleeding from the gunshot wound. A knot rising on her forehead. Her eyes closed.

He rushed to her side. "Kate, I'm here. Hang on. You have to hang on for me." The fear in his voice wouldn't go away. He squeezed her limp, cold hand.

Her eyelids flew open and she stared into his eyes. A single tear slipped onto her neck before she collapsed, unconscious.

"We have to get her to the emergency room right away," the doctor said, and he and a nurse took Kate away.

Brady turned to Aamon. How could this have happened so soon? The guilt he felt for not protecting her was a bitter pill.

"What happened?"

Aamon pointed to a quiet corner of the hospital. "Let's talk there."

Numb, Brady followed.

"She was barely hanging on when I found her. I wasn't able to get much out, except that someone had run her off the road. Kate was pretty sure the man who shot her was that Ward person."

"Do we know what kind of vehicle he's driving?"

Aamon shook his head. "From what I can tell from the tracks, it was some type of large truck or SUV. Hopefully, Kate can give us more to go on." Aamon shook his head. "If it wasn't for her dog, she'd probably be dead right now."

Brady shot him a look. "What do you mean?"

"Callie ran all the way from the wreck to where I was parked, barking like crazy and pawing at my patrol vehicle. I knew right away something was wrong. When the dog took off running, I followed. That's when I saw Kate. She'd tried to walk back to the house, but she didn't make it."

Amazed, Brady couldn't believe Kate's bravery or the dog's. Kate owed Callie her life.

"Where is the dog now?" he asked.

"In my vehicle. She was pretty worked up on the ride here. She kept licking Kate's face."

"She loves her master." The story was nothing short of a miracle. Brady shook his head. "I feel so helpless. I don't know what to do to help."

Aamon patted his arm. "Why don't you wait for news from her doctor? Then be with her. Maybe once she's treated she'll remember something that will help us find who attacked her. I'm going out to see if I can take a better look at the wreck. Frank and Maddie were heading that way when I called earlier." Maddie Cooper was the newest deputy in the county. She'd moved out west from New York last year.

Brady nodded. "Let me know what you find out. You want to put the dog in my SUV?"

"I'll do it. Call me when she's awake. Tell her I'm praying for her."

"Will do." After Aamon left, he found a chair close to the place where the doctor had taken Kate. The hospital was thriving with activity and he watched as medical personnel hurried past.

He needed stillness in his being, and there was

only one way to find that. Brady lowered his head and prayed for Kate.

Please, bring her out of this safely. Heal her, Lord. Don't let her die because of my mistakes.

"Deputy?" Brady glanced up and saw Kate's doctor standing near him.

Brady shot to his feet. "Is she okay?" he asked, his voice unsteady.

The doctor smiled briefly. "She's going to be. From what I hear, that's one smart dog she has."

Brady's worry melted into a smile. "She is. Can I see Kate?"

The doctor nodded. "Yes, in fact, she's been asking for you. I thought you'd like to know, we pulled a 38-caliber bullet out of Kate's arm. Hope that will help with your investigation. She's this way."

He followed the doctor into the emergency room. The doctor opened one of the curtained areas where Kate lay on a bed. The sight of her looking so pale tore at his heart. It was a struggle to keep it together.

Brady approached her bedside and took her hand. "How are you feeling?" Her green eyes were huge against pale skin.

"I've felt better." She managed a smile that disappeared. "Where's Callie?"

"She's fine. She's in my SUV. Remind me to give Callie a whole bunch of treats when this is over. She saved your life."

Tears rimmed her eyes. "I know."

The doctor cleared his throat. "I'll leave you two alone. Try not to tire her too much, Deputy?"

Brady's full attention never left Kate. There were so many things he needed to say to her, but right now he needed to work the case because her life was still in jeopardy.

"Do you feel like talking about what happened?"

She managed a nod. "I saw a vehicle approaching fast. A large SUV." Her gaze held his. "They didn't slow down and rammed the truck hard. I hit my head." She touched the knot on her forehead. "The next thing I remember was waking up in the river. The water was rushing inside the cab. I managed to get both Callie and myself out in time." She shuddered as she recalled the incident.

"I told Callie to go for help. Then I saw two men on the bridge. I felt a shot in my arm and went under. When I surfaced, I heard a voice. It was Steve Ward's voice. He's the one who shot me. Then he and his partner left. They didn't think I'd survive. They left me there to die."

Brady sat down on the bed and gathered her close. She was trembling as she recalled the incident.

After a moment, she pulled away and he let her go, brushing back hair from her face. "This is helpful. I'll call and let Aamon know. He and another deputy along with our sheriff are at the wreck scene now." He started to rise when she grabbed his hand.

"Thank you," she murmured and his own guilt twisted on his face.

"Don't thank me. I should have seen this coming and done something about it. I shouldn't have let you out of my sight."

She shook her head. "No, you couldn't have foreseen this happening, but I should have. I should have just kept running when I saw the light out back. I knew something was up, but I didn't want to accept it."

He sat back down. "No, Kate, you did the right thing. You can't keep running all your life, and you deserve to be happy. A second chance at life. And I'm going to do everything in my power to make sure that happens."

She sucked in a breath, the look in her eyes hopeful. He was mesmerized by what he saw there. More than anything, he longed to lower his lips to hers and kiss her. He'd been living above the surface for years. His high school sweetheart had broken his heart, and since that time, he'd been too wounded to try for another serious relationship, drifting from one superficial connection to another. Kate made him want more. He wanted all of her.

As if reading his mind, she leaned forward and claimed his lips, her touch gentle, exciting, taking him off guard.

He froze for a second, then kissed her back with all the emotions that had gathered inside him since the day he met her. He wanted the nightmare to end for her. Wanted to be part of her future.

Kate broke away, her eyes wide. She stared at him for a moment, then burst out laughing. "I'm sorry. I don't know what came over me."

He joined in her laughter. "I'm glad you did because I really wanted to. I just thought the timing might be a little off.

Her expression sobered. "I've wanted to as well." Her lips were swollen from the kiss. He leaned over and gently touched his to hers again. A tender kiss filled with promise.

A breath separated them. He cupped her cheek, his eyes clinging to hers. The sound of shuffling feet nearby made Brady pull.

He shot to his feet and faced the doctor who had slipped inside without them realizing it.

"Sorry to interrupt, but I just wanted to check on my patient."

"Of course, I'll give you some privacy." With a quick look Kate's way, he slipped from the space.

With his hands trembling, he called Aamon, needing a distraction.

"How's Kate?" Aamon asked the minute he answered.

"She's awake. I was able to talk to her a bit, and she believes the vehicle that ran her off the road was an SUV. She confirmed that Ward was the person who shot her. Oh, and she was shot with a 38."

"That gives us something to go on anyway."

"Yep. What's new there?" Brady asked, hoping they had some leads.

"Nothing really. Some tire tracks heading toward town. Maddie's checking them out. We pulled the truck out of the river. I'm afraid it's totaled, along with most of Kate's possessions. We managed to recover some paperwork. I was thinking its work-related."

Brady waited until a nurse passed by. He noticed the doctor standing near the curtained area where Kate was, no doubt waiting for him. "Hold onto it for me. We're going to need it."

"Will do. If we find anything useful, I'll let you know."

"Thanks, buddy. I'll talk to you soon." Brady ended the call and headed to where the doctor stood.

"Anything wrong?" he asked at the frown on the doctor's face.

"She wants to leave the hospital today. Right now, in fact. I don't recommend it. I'd like to keep her for observation overnight."

Brady knew the doctor was being cautious, but he had a feeling Kate's mind was made up.

"I'll see if I can change her mind," he said and stepped into the space again. She was sitting on the edge of the bed. "Kate, what are you doing? You need to rest. You almost died."

She shook her head. "He told me the same thing." She grabbed her clothes from where they lay. "He's still out there, and he's killed a lot of people. We have to find him."

He steadied her when she rose to her feet. "We will, but you need to rest."

She shook her head. "He thinks I'm dead for now. We have breathing room. I'll be fine."

It was pointless to argue. "All right. Are you able to get dressed by yourself?"

"I think so. Can you get the doctor on the same page?" He smiled at her choice of words. She might not be part of the Agency anymore, but she hadn't forgotten her training.

"I will. Get dressed. I'm springing you from this place."

~

Callie bounded to the front seat and into her lap. Kate winced in pain, rubbing the dog's head.

"Whoa there, Callie," Brady said. "Be gentle on your master."

Callie sniffed Kate's arm, then settled down in the back seat.

Once Brady pulled out onto the main road, he said, "I'm afraid all your things were ruined by the water."

Her eyes darted to him. "Tony's file."

"Aamon has it. Most of the pages got wet, but he's going to dry them. I think they're still legible."

She breathed out a sigh. "We need them. There has to be answers in there somewhere."

"I spoke to Aamon. He was heading to the station. I'll stop by and grab the file. I'm afraid you may need some new clothes though."

Kate stared down at her damp, stained jeans and plaid shirt. "Is there someplace in town where I can pick up some necessary things...My purse! Everything—my ID and money—everything is in there."

He clasped her hand. "I'll check with Aamon. I'm sure he has them."

She nodded and watched as the town came into view. He pulled in front of the station, then turned to her. "I don't want to leave you alone."

She loved the way he cared for her. "I'll come with you." She turned to the dog. "Stay, Callie. We'll be right back." The dog reluctantly lay back down.

Brady got out and she did the same. Her head

felt as if someone were playing drums inside, and her arm ached from the bullet wound. She had several bruised ribs, but she was alive, praise God. Everything else would heal.

He held the door open for her and together they went inside. Four people were talking quietly. She recognized Aamon. The other man and two women she did not. When she and Brady came into the room, the conversation stopped.

"You're out of the hospital already?" Aamon exclaimed.

Kate nodded. "Yes. Thank you for saving my life." She went to where he stood and gave him a hug.

"You're welcome, but I think all the thanks go to Callie. She's some dog."

She smiled. "She is at that."

Aamon pointed to the older man who wore a sheriff's badge and the younger woman blonde standing next to him. "Kate, this is Sheriff Frank Lawson and Deputy Maddie Cooper."

Kate shook both their hands. "It's nice to meet you. I appreciate your help."

"You're welcome," the sheriff told her.

"And this is Jenny Newton. The place wouldn't run without Jenny."

The older redhead waved her hand in front of her, dismissing Aamon's praise. "It's a pleasure to meet you, Kate. It's too bad it has to be under these circumstances."

Kate smiled at the woman. They all seemed like nice people and she'd upset their world in a few days.

"I have your papers. I managed to get them dried." Aamon went to one of the desks and shuffled papers together, then handed them to her. "Oh, and we recovered your purse as well."

"Thank you," she said, relieved and grateful at the same time.

With all eyes on her, she thought of the scar on her face and fought against the impulse to hide it.

"Are there any new developments?" Brady asked, no doubt sensing her unease.

"Nothing yet," the sheriff told him. "Maddie followed the SUV's tracks. They headed to Lone Wolf. If these guys believe Kate's dead, they may be long gone by now."

If only, Kate thought.

"I'm taking Kate to my house," Brady told his colleagues. "She can't go back to her place."

The sheriff nodded. "That's a good idea. Until we find these guys or know for sure they're gone, it's best to stay out of sight."

"Thank you all," Kate told them. She had been on her own for so long. Accepting help was hard to do, but she knew she had no choice.

As they passed the spot where the accident had happened, Kate couldn't help but shudder at how close to death she'd come. She reached back and patted Callie's head. The dog was loyal beyond belief.

Brady glanced up at the darkening sky. "The storm's coming in fast. I'm glad we don't have far to go."

Already, the snow had begun to fall harder, making it hard to see much beyond the hood of the

SUV.

They drove past her entrance and Brady slowed at what appeared to be fresh tire tracks heading up the drive.

"Someone's been there," she managed as he sped past the place. Once they were a safe distance, he grabbed his cell phone. "Aamon, someone's been up to Kate's place since you left."

After a moment's pause, Brady spoke again. "Okay, let me know what you find."

"Do you think they've come back?" she asked, but it didn't make sense. They thought she was dead. Why come back to her house and risk being captured?

"I'm not sure. Until we know what we're up against, we can't dismiss anything."

They drove in silence for a while, and then Brady turned into a gated entrance that read Connors Ranch. "This is it." He headed down the paved drive. "My dad lives in the main house off to the right. I built my own place several years back. I've let my dad know we're coming. I wanted him to be aware of what is happening, just in case."

She smiled at him and gently touched his arm. "That's a good idea. I just hope those guys don't come after him."

Brady smiled and shook his head. "Don't worry about Dad. He can take care of himself. That man is as tough as they get."

The SUV entered a wooded area off to the left. Kate loved the way the trees were covered in snow, giving it a magical feel. Up ahead, she spotted a rambling, two-story log home. Brady pulled into the circular drive and stopped. "This is home."

He grabbed the bag containing the clothes she'd purchased at the general store and climbed out. He came around to Kate's door and opened it. "It's really coming down now. Let's get inside."

Kate followed him up to the front porch with Callie at her heels. Even though it was hard to see much through the thickening snowfall, the place was idyllic. The snow-covered woods set a charming background for the majestic log cabin.

"I should warn you, I have three dogs of my own, and they can be quite enthusiastic. But don't worry, they're going to love you."

Brady slid the key into the lock and held the door open for her. Callie bounded through the door and skidded to an abrupt halt when three dogs of various sizes jumped from the nearby sofa and approached to investigate their new arrival.

All three dogs were smaller than Callie and happy to have a visitor. They jumped around her, wagging their tails. Poor Callie didn't know what to think.

"Jake, Sophie, Tyson, that's enough." He shooed them away from Callie.

"It's okay, they're just getting to know each other, and we are in their territory," Kate said with a smile.

The dogs, spotting Kate for the first time, hurried toward her to sniff her clothes. She bent down and patted each of their heads. "They precious." The dogs were all mixed. One had a scar on his leg.

"That's Jake, he's the newest. I found him on

the road. Hit and run. Busted up his back leg pretty good."

She lovingly ran her fingers through Jake's and the other dog's fur, then glanced up at Brady. "They're all rescue animals?"

He nodded. "Sophie here was abandoned. I found her when I went to investigate a possible meth lab. We arrived too late to stop the lab, but Sophie was there alone so I brought her home. And Tyson here." He gathered the smallest dog in his arms. "Well, I found him out in the cold behind the station. I think someone dumped him there. Maybe they figured we'd find a good home for him."

She loved that he cared so much about animals. "I think you did find a good home for him."

He chuckled and set the dog down. "Come on guys, let's get you dinner. Callie, you might as well join the meal. I'll get an extra bowl."

With the dogs getting along well enough, Kate surveyed the cabin's interior. It had a distinct western theme. An antler chandelier hung from the twenty-foot aspen ceiling. The walls sported artwork depicting cowboys in various poses at different seasons of the year. A rich, chocolate-leather sofa and matching chairs faced the fireplace that was in the middle of a wall of windows, reflecting the growing storm and a mountain in the distance.

The kitchen, great room and dining area all flowed together to give a feeling of immense space.

"Your home is beautiful, Brady."

"Thanks. I'd like to say I did it all myself, but my mom helped with the interior decorating before she passed away."

She had no idea his mother was deceased. "I'm so sorry. How long has she been gone?"

"Going on four years now. It's still hard not seeing her there with my dad."

Kate understood loss. She'd lost Tony and several of her comrades, but before that when she was away at college, her parents had died in a car accident. "It's hard, isn't it? Losing someone you love?"

"It is." He gazed at her for the longest time, then slowly came closer. When he was inches away, he smoothed errant strands of hair from her face, then gently stroked the scar on her cheek. She shuddered at his touch and fought not to pull away. "Did you get this when your partner and team were killed?"

She swallowed visibly. "Yes. Everyone else died, yet I lived. Even today, I don't know why."

He leaned in and kissed the scar, then stared at her through the inches separating them. "There has to be a reason. There always is. Maybe you were spared to bring this madman to justice."

Tears rimmed her eyes. "Maybe so."

"Let me help you bring whoever is behind this to justice, for their sakes."

Through tears, she managed a smile. "I'd like that."

Brady tipped her chin back and kissed her lips, his touch grazing her skin. She felt it to her core. Her world, tipped on its edge, righting itself.

Slowly, he let her go, his breath labored like hers. "I should check in with Aamon. See what he found at your place." Yet he didn't move. His gaze remained tangled with hers, and her heart soared. A bit of hope lightened the dark future she'd come to fear.

Brady stepped away and retrieved his phone from his pocket. Kate turned, gathering air into her lungs. She was falling hard. The thought of love amazed her. Even though it was the worst possible time, she was falling for Brady and nothing her head told her made any difference.

"All right, thanks, Aamon. Try to stay warm. The weather's going to be a bugger."

Once he'd finished the call, Kate steeled herself to face him again.

"Aamon checked your place. Someone was there. They broke into the house through one of the living room windows. The place was tossed. He's parked his cruiser at Sarah's place to keep an eye on the house in case whoever was there comes back."

Kate glanced past Brady at the darkening skies outside. Snow mixed with pellets of ice continued to torment the windows. A storm was on the way and she wasn't sure she could handle another one. She'd waited through six long years to meet the face behind the nightmare. Was she ready to confront the man who had destroyed so many lives?

Chapter Eight

Kate glanced up from the meal they'd prepared together, her gaze returning to the storm raging outside the window.

He wished that he could reassure her everything was going to be okay, but nothing was further from the truth.

She pushed her plate away. Like him, her appetite wasn't there.

"How about some coffee?' he asked to draw her attention from the danger outside.

Her gaze met his and she sighed. "That sounds good."

Once they finished clearing away the meal, Brady made coffee. He could feel her restlessness—the way her eyes darted toward the door at the slightest sound, the way her foot tapped against the table.

"Do you remember the number of your contact?" he asked. Her phone had been destroyed by water. So far, nothing in her partner's notes shined a beacon on the killer.

She nodded. "Yes, I do."

He handed her his phone. "Try him again." She took the phone and dialed the number. It was only a second before she had her answer.

"Straight to voice mail."

He didn't like it. With so grave a situation, why wouldn't her former commander return her calls...unless he couldn't?

Brady glanced down at the papers they'd been working on. "Is there anyone else you can go to at the Agency?"

Her expression cleared. "Yes. Mark Franklin. In fact, I contacted him when I couldn't reach Jon. I'll try him now."

Kate dialed the number and motioned him closer, putting the phone on speaker.

"Mark, it's Sidney." She glanced at Brady. Hearing her use another name was jarring. "Have you been able to reach Jon yet?"

The audible sigh was unsettling. "Sid, am I glad you called. I haven't heard from Jon. In fact, I was so worried when he didn't call back I went to his place yesterday. Sid, there was signs of a struggle and blood. I'm worried. I have a team set up. They're going over his place and his computer to see if anything comes up."

Kate turned as white as the sweater around her shoulders. "Let me know when you have anything, Mark. No matter the time."

"I will. I don't like it, Sid. I don't like it at all."

Kate ended the call. Her hands were shaking. Brady clasped them in his, forcing her attention to him.

"We don't know what's happened yet. We

can't jump to conclusions until we do."

She managed a nod. "I know," she breathed the word out. "I'm just so worried about him."

"We'll figure it out." As much as he wanted to be the one to bring this nightmare to an end, he felt as if he were groping in the dark.

Brady brought her hand to his lips and kissed her palm. "Coffee's ready. I'll pour you a cup."

She rose. "Let me help. I need something to take my mind off Jon."

Brady poured two cups and handed her one. "Let's go over the facts as we know them, starting at the beginning. Maybe something will come to mind."

"Okay." She eyed him skeptically as she sipped her coffee.

"How did you first get onto this arms dealer?"

She considered the question for a moment. "Through one of Tony's asset. He had dozens of them. Tony knew how to gain trust."

Although she'd never said as much, Brady sensed that there was more between Kate and Tony.

"He sounds like a smart guy." He waited for her to add more.

She smiled and clasped his hand. "He was. I loved him," she admitted, her words a knife to his heart. "It seems like such a long time ago now."

"I'm sorry you lost him." As much as it hurt to think of her being in love, he understood. He'd been crazy about Heather. As high school sweethearts, he thought they had a future together. Then the summer after graduation, she told him it was over. She wanted her freedom. Wanted to experience college life without being tied to someone. The breakup hurt like crazy.

"Tony was always so full of life and I'll always care for him, but he wouldn't want me to mourn forever. He would tell me to find out who killed him and move on."

Brady returned his smile. "He sounds like a wise man. I think I would like him."

"And he would like you."

Brady gathered his straying thoughts. "What can you tell me about this asset?"

Kate glanced out at the storm raging. "She's a female. Tony guarded his assets closely, but there is a picture of her." She dug through the documents they'd spread out on the coffee table, and handed the photo to him. "It's not much to go on."

He studied the picture. The woman was barely visible. The photographer had captured her from the side. She had dark hair pulled back into a ponytail. Her features appeared European.

"What did Tony tell you about this guy you were chasing?"

"Only that he was new to the game. His asset said that he was moving large amounts of weapons across Europe." She shook her head. "We caught up with him in Germany, or so we thought, but we were too late. It was the same for more than two years. We'd track him down only to discover we'd just missed him."

Brady wondered about the reliability of the asset. "How'd you end up in that D.C. warehouse?"

She focused somewhere beyond his shoulder, peering into the past. "We thought we'd lost his trail. It had been months with no word, then out of the blue, he popped up in the States, according to Tony's asset. She was embedded with the smuggler somehow. Anyway, she gave us the location of the warehouse...only when we arrived, it was a setup. The rest of the team went in first," she murmured, her eyes distant. "Then Tony and me. The place was wired to explode. Tony realized it. He turned to me." She stopped to gather air. "He told me to run, then shoved me hard. I thought he was right behind me." Tears gathered in her eyes, spilling over, as if she were reliving it. "I didn't make it out before the place went up like a rocket. The next thing I remember was waking up in the hospital and being told Tony and the rest of my team were dead."

Brady couldn't imagine the pain she carried with her. The guilt of being the only one who walked out of that warehouse alive.

He pulled her closer. "I'm so sorry," he whispered. Her body quaked with spent emotion. He held her while she cried, and he prayed that one day the horrible things would become a distant memory, and he could be there with her and hopefully become worthy of her love.

~

Scrubbing tears away, she peered into his eyes. Unable to deny the truth any longer, Kate realized she didn't want to.

She gently touched his face, then leaned her forehead against his. "Thank you for being here for me. No matter the outcome, I'm grateful."

The warmth of him close held a promise for the future, but she couldn't let herself grab onto it just yet.

"You're welcome. I'll always be there for you, if you want me to be."

A smile lifted the corners of her lips when she looked at him. "I do."

"But there are things that need to be finished first." He said what she could not.

She pulled away, regret seeping into her smile. "Yes. I have to find out what happened at that warehouse—for Tony and my friends."

"Then let's finish this thing once and for all."

Kate leaned in and touched her lips to his, then rose. "Let's keep going over the files. Talking it out is helping."

She grabbed his cup and refilled both his and hers.

"What happened after the explosion?" he asked while accepting the refill with a smile.

Remembering that dark time was hard. "I was in the hospital for almost two weeks. I was in pretty bad shape. Jon was there just about every day and when he wasn't, armed men stood guard." She drew in a breath. She'd been in and out of consciousness. "When I was able to leave the hospital, Jon told me that I was in danger. I couldn't go back to work. Ever. There were numerous attempts to gain access to me at the hospital. I knew then that I was done with the CIA. Jon helped me stage the accident scene." She snatched a look at Brady. "And so, Sidney Michaels died that day." She shook her head. "Since then, I've changed my name half a dozen times, each one after being found out. I don't know how this guy keeps finding me, but I do know he's good and he'll keep coming until one of us is dead."

Brady clasped her hand. "I'm not going to let him hurt you. This thing, whatever it is, ends here."

His confidence was admirable, but he didn't know what they were up against. The man who killed her team was cunning and patient. He'd spent six years tracking her down.

Brady's cell phone rang. He answered, but said nothing at first, his eyes widening with every passing second. "Are you sure?" He listened for a moment longer, then said, "I'll check it out."

He ended the call, his gaze locking with hers. "That was my dad. Once of the alarms went off on the south side of his place. It could just be the wind or an animal…"

"But you don't believe that."

"No, I don't. I'm going to check it out, but first I want to call in the cavalry. I don't like the way this feels."

He turned away to make the call, missing the shudder that ran through her. Her bad feeling doubled.

"Okay, Sheriff. We'll see you soon." He faced her again. "That was Frank. He doesn't want us to leave the house until he and the rest of the team arrive." He shook his head. "That's probably a good idea. I'll call my dad back and tell him what's happening."

She went over to the fire, holding her hands in front of it. In the windows, darkness reflected back the room. She felt like an animal on display in the zoo. Brady must have sensed her unease because he took out a remote control and clicked a button. All the window shades lowered.

Kate faced him. "Thank you."

"No problem." He came over to where she stood. "Dad says there's been no further incidents. Let's hope it's just the wind." The taut set of his jaw told her he didn't believe it either.

Outside, the sound of multiple vehicles coming their way had Brady inching toward the window. "It's the sheriff and the rest of the team."

Relief made her knees weak. They weren't alone any longer. They had help.

Brady pulled the door open and the sheriff, Aamon, and Deputy Maddie Cooper came inside. Brady relocked the door.

"Kate," the sheriff acknowledged her. "Has anything else happened?"

Brady shook his head. "No, nothing. I spoke to Dad. The alarm hasn't gone off again."

"Let's take a look around to be sure." He nodded toward Maddie. "Why don't you stay here with Kate? We'll be right back."

"No, I'm coming with you, Sheriff. This is my life. They want me."

Frank pinned her with a piercing look. "All right, but you stick close to Brady, and you don't go off on your own."

She nodded and grabbed her coat along with her Glock. Callie jumped to her feet, ready to follow.

"Stay, Callie." She waited until the dog grudgingly sat before she patted her head. "I'll be right back."

With flashlights in hand, the five of them headed out into the teeth of the storm, unsure of what they would find.

"Dad said it was the sensor to the south of the house," Brady told the team.

"Let's start there. We can fan it out from that point."

As they headed to the back of the main house, Kate couldn't dismiss the feeling that they were being stalked, their predator waiting for just the right moment to pounce.

Chapter Nine

Brady could feel the intensity of the storm continue to grow. Just putting one foot in front of the other was a near impossible feat. The flashlight barely penetrated the sheets of snow that sliced through them. The temperature was in sub-zero numbers. If they lingered out here long, frostbite was a real possibility.

Once they arrived at the spot where the sensor had gone off, his dad, Zeke Connors, stepped onto the porch and hurried down to meet them.

"Frank," his dad greeted his good friend, then acknowledged the rest of the team with a nod. "As I told Brady, there's been no further incidents. I'm guessing the wind set it off. It's really howling tonight."

Standing upright amongst the gusts was hard. Snow covered each of them. Brady couldn't remember the last time they'd taken a beating from a storm like this one.

Something caught Brady's attention and he shined the flashlight on the area, his heart plummeting. Footsteps. One set.

"Sheriff, look at this." Brady called them over.

"Zeke, you should go back inside," Frank told his friend.

Once his father had reluctantly closed the door behind him, Frank said, "Let's fan out. Aamon, you come with me. Maddie, go with Brady and Kate. While it appears there's only one person out here, it could be a trick." Frank glanced around the group. "Stay on your toes."

The footprints were all over the back side of the house. Some partially covered with snow. Others almost hidden.

Frank and Aamon disappeared around the side of the house, while Brady, Kate, and Maddie headed toward the woods out back.

Brady had been on many hunts to bring down bad guys. He'd faced down some evil men in his time, but his nerves were screaming to alert like never before. Nothing from his past had prepared him for this. Sheer terror filled him for Kate. What if they failed and couldn't keep her safe?

"It's hard to see anything in this storm." Kate's words were barely audible.

"It's growing stronger. We can't stay out here too much longer," Maddie warned.

Brady felt helpless. Where had the guy gone? They were so close. They needed to find him now, before he could do any more damage.

"What's that over there?" Maddie pointed her flashlight a dark figure. They battled the fierce wind to the spot.

A man lay huddled in the cold. "Get your hands in the air," Brady ordered.

The man moved in slow motion. He lifted his hands, then jerked toward them.

Kate gasped, then knelt next to the man. "Jon? What are you doing out here?"

Shocked, Brady was at her side in a second. This was Kate's commander?

"Let's get him inside." Brady called Frank's number, knowing it would be impossible for the sheriff to hear them call out in the raging storm.

"We have Kate's commander. It looks as if he's hurt. We're taking him inside my dad's house."

Kate put her arm around the man with Brady's help. They hoisted him to his feet while Maddie hurried ahead and pounded on the back door.

Zeke pulled the door open, saw the man, and opened it wide. "Come inside."

Frank and Aamon arrived and with Kate's help, they helped the man to the sofa near the fireplace.

"We need to get you warmed up," Kate told Jon.

He was shivering. Blood seeped through his jacket.

"He's injured. Let me have a look," Zeke told them. As a retired physician, it was a lucky break for the man. "Brady, help me get his jacket off."

Easing the bloodied materiel from his injured arm was difficult. Every little move made him wince in pain.

Once they'd freed him of the jacket, Zeke cut the shirt sleeve free of the wound and sat back in alarm. The wound wasn't recent, and it hadn't been treated.

Jon drifted in and out of consciousness.

Once Zeke cleaned the wound, Brady realized that while he was definitely shot, it was a grazing wound.

Thank You, God.

"He's suffering from the beginnings of hypothermia. You found him just in time. He should be fine once he gets warm and has some rest," Zeke told them.

Which meant they'd have to wait to question him.

"What was he doing out there alone?" Kate asked. "How did he find me?"

Brady had more questions than answers, but he had a bad feeling that this was just beginning of a very long night.

"I'm guessing he was trying to warn you. Whoever shot him didn't want that to happen."

"You he found me again?" The weight of those words on her was hard to take.

Brady went to her and squeezed her arm. "We'll get him. This is almost over." While she managed a smile, she didn't believe him.

"Kate?" Startled, Kate hurried to the man's side. He looked much better. More alert. He glanced around the room, startled. "What's happening?"

Kate sat next to him. "You've been shot, Jon. How did you get here?"

Jon drew in a weak breath. "I tracked your phone. I found out that your location was compromised, and I had to warn you…only he and his goons came after me. He wanted me to lead them to you. I refused. They shot me in the arm and left me for dead."

Kate hugged the man close. "I'm so sorry you had to go through that, but you're safe now."

In an instant, Brady was on alert. His father said the wound was superficial. Why would the men chasing Kate leave an eyewitness who could identify them alive? And why was the man out there in the storm? If he'd walked from the main road, wouldn't he be in worse shape than he was? Something about his story didn't add up in Brady's mind.

~

Kate glanced up at Brady and saw his brow knitted together in a frown. Something was wrong.

"Rest now," she told Jon, and then rose and approached Brady. "What is it?" she asked, worried by what she saw on his face.

"I'm not sure. Something about his story doesn't add up." He pulled her aside and whispered his suspicions.

Her heart wouldn't let her go there. "You're wrong. I know Jon. He saved my life." Yet Brady clearly wasn't convinced.

She glanced back at Jon. He was eyeing the people around him, his manner nervous. Was it possible?

Before she could say a word, a dog barked outside. She recognized the sound of it. "That's Callie," she said and hurried toward the sound.

Brady went after her. "Kate, wait."

Callie continued to bark ferociously. "She has something."

"Maddie, stay here," Frank told his deputy. He and Aamon followed Brady and Kate outside.

84

They'd barely cleared the door when they were ambushed by multiple gunshots.

Behind them, a single gun fired. With weapons drawn, they kept as low as they could and edged back inside.

Jon was on his feet, a weapon in his hand. Maddie lay on the floor close by. Blood spewed from her shoulder.

"That's far enough," Jon warned, pointing the weapon at Kate. She couldn't process what she saw. "Get your hands in the air."

Five armed men pushed their way inside, seizing their weapons.

"Jon, what did you do?" she asked, reality beginning to hit her. Jon, the man she'd trusted completely, was the one behind the deaths of so many agents.

"You wouldn't let it go, would you? I didn't want to have to do this. If you'd just kept to yourself none of this would have happened, but you couldn't let it go, could you?" The rage on his face was hard to associate with the man she knew and loved.

"Why?" Slowly the truth dawned. Jon was the man they'd been chasing for the past six years. Jon was the weapon's dealer.

"She needs help. Let me take a look at her," Zeke urged.

Jon pointed the gun at Zeke. "Do what you can, but you're not using any instruments. I don't trust you."

Zeke nodded. "I'll need help. My son." He pointed to Brady.

Jon's gaze shot between Zeke and Brady. "Fine, but I'm warning you, if you try anything, she'll be dead before you know it."

Jon moved closer to Kate. The barrel of the gun inches from her temple.

Her thoughts flew into a dozen directions, but she tried to pull them together. She needed answers. If she was going to die here, she needed answers. "What happened to Tony's asset?"

Jon's grin had a maniacal edge to it. "You mean my asset. She worked for me, helping me coordinate the shipments, until I found out she'd started talking to Tony. I knew it was only a matter of time before she discovered the truth and ratted me out to Tony, so I had to use a little persuasion. She had a family. I told her if she wanted to see them alive again, she'd do exactly what I told her to do. So she scheduled a series of 'near-misses' to make Tony believe she was trustworthy."

It had all been a setup. "The warehouse. She told Tony you'd be there, only you had other plans. You took out the entire team to save yourself some prison time." The pain searing through her was hard to bear.

"I had no choice. You know what they do to traitors. I thought I was in the clear until I found out you'd lived, thanks to Tony's chivalry." Jon shook his head in disgust. "But I liked you, so I figured I'd keep an eye on you. Make sure you behaved."

"The threats. They were all bogus. You shot yourself to make it appear you'd been captured."

He didn't look surprised. "That's right."

"What did you do to Tony's asset?"

He glared at her. "What do you think? She'd served her purpose. I killed her and disposed of her body. Just like I'm going to do with you. It's just too bad you had to get these nice people involved in your problems, Sidney. Now they have to die as well." He motioned to the men standing behind Frank and Aamon. They grabbed them by the arms. Two other men stood close to Brady and Zeke. Kate met Brady's gaze. Saw him motion toward the men close to them. They had to try to disarm the men. She'd need to do the same with Jon. It was their only chance.

Out of the corner of her eye, Kate noticed the door stood open. Callie was just outside, her hair standing at attention watching Jon as if waiting her command. Did she dare?

"Callie, attack," she yelled, then grabbed at the weapon in Jon's hand. While they struggled, she became aware of the same thing happening around her. Callie leapt through the air and grabbed Jon's injured arm. He screamed in pain and let go of the weapon, trying to fight the dog off, but Callie was ferocious, defending her master. Ironically, Jon was the one who had given her the dog.

With Callie latched onto Jon's arm, he dropped to his knees, cowering. Kate snatched the weapon and fired close to the men struggling with Aamon and the sheriff. The men stopped at its sound.

Kate trained the gun on them. "That's enough. Drop your weapons and get your hands in the air or the next shot hits flesh."

Slowly both men obeyed. Aamon and Frank

gathered their weapons. She turned to Brady. He'd managed to retrieve Maddie's weapon and had one of the men disarmed. The second had his weapon pointed at Zeke, ready to shoot. Brady fired once. The man dropped to his knees. The gun flying from his bloodied hand. Zeke rushed to secure it.

"Release, Callie," she ordered, and the dog reluctantly let Jon go, but stayed crouched close by, ready to attack again. Callie had saved her life. Again. She knelt next to the dog and hugged her close while Callie wagged her tail. "I love you, baby girl. You did good." Callie licked her face in response.

In no time, all the men were cuffed including Jon, and Brady called an ambulance for Maddie and the other injured men.

"I need to call Mark. He can send help." Brady handed her his phone and she called her former comrade.

Mark was in shock once she'd finished giving him the details.

"I'll send a team immediately. I'm just glad everyone's okay, Sidney."

While she was fine, she was shell-shocked by what took place. She'd waited six years to put a face to the monster who had claimed so many lives, only to find it was one of her own.

"I say let's get these guys to the station and in jail. It's going to be a long night."

"I'll be right behind you," Brady told the team as they led the prisoners away.

"Sure thing," Frank told him. "Zeke, do you mind coming with us? I'll want to get your statement on file."

When it was just the two of them, with Callie sticking close to her side, she faced Brady. The uncertainty in his eyes tore at her heart. She knew exactly what was troubling him.

"It's finally over, Kate...I mean Sidney. That's going to take some getting used to. But you don't have to hide anymore." He touched her face and she snuggled his hand.

"No more hiding." She smiled with her heart in her eyes. "Only good things ahead."

"Any idea what you plan to do next? Will you go back to the CIA?" She could tell how hard that question was to ask, and she needed to assure him.

"No, I'm done with that life. The things I've done in the name of justice." She shook her head. "I want to put that all in the past. For the first time in six years, I have a future and I can't think of any place I'd rather be than right here in Soaring Eagle." She wrapped her arms around his neck. "Or anyone else I'd like to share it with than you, Brady Connors."

His face broke into a smile and he took her in his arms and kissed her. And for once, the future looked as promising as the smile on Brady's face.

Epilogue

Six months later…

"Ready, Sidney?" her future father-in-law asked. "You look lovely."

Sidney smiled at Zeke. "Yes, I'm ready. I can't believe I'm getting married. I'm the luckiest woman in the world. I love your son so much."

Zeke chuckled. "Oh, I don't know. I think my son's pretty lucky, too. He picked a winner. You're a strong woman, Sidney, and Brady loves you."

Sidney wasn't sure how Zeke would react when she asked him to walk her down the aisle, but the senior Connors was brought to tears. He told her he was so thankful that she'd chosen their little slice of heaven to run away to, but for Sidney, she knew it was more than an accident. It was Tony who guided her here. While they dated, he'd told her stories about growing up in the wide-open spaces of Wyoming. He'd made it sound so perfect, she had to see for herself. In the process, she'd finally located the man responsible for Tony's and the rest of the team's deaths and found the love of her life.

Thank you, Tony.

"Let's do this," she whispered, and then knelt in front of Callie. "Ready, girl?"

The dog wagged her tail.

"Go find Brady."

The dog hurried down the aisle. The pouch containing their wedding rings tied around her neck.

Zeke chuckled, and she glanced at him, questions in her eyes.

"It's just that if you'd told me my son would be getting married to a former CIA agent and that the ring bearer would be a dog, I'd said you had too much to drink."

She joined in laughing, her eyes shining with happiness.

"It's pretty crazy-sounding, I'll give you that."

They reached the door of the sanctuary where Brady told her he'd gone to church since he was a little boy. Sidney couldn't think of a better place to make him her husband. Her heart overflowed with love, the future brighter than it had been in a long time.

Maddie, completely healed from her gunshot wound, was Sidney's only bridesmaid. Maddie finished her walk down the aisle and the wedding march began.

"This is it," she said as Brady glanced up and their eyes met. Held. Her future was right there in front of her to grasp, and she was ready. Oh, she was ready.

The End

About The Author

Mary Alford grew up in a small Texas town famous for, well not much of anything, really. Being the baby of the family and quite a bit younger than her brothers and sisters, Mary had plenty of time to entertain herself. Making up stories seem to come natural to her.

As a pre-teen, Mary discovered Christian Suspense and knew instinctively that was what she wanted to do with her over-active imagination.

She wrote her first novel as a teen, (it's tucked away somewhere never to see the light of day), but never really pursued her writing career seriously until a few years later, when she wrote her first romance and was hooked.

Today, Mary still lives in Texas, and still writes about romance. In fact, she can't think of anything else she'd rather do.

You can find out more about Mary's work on her website, www.maryalford.net. And be sure to check out these books by Mary.

Nowhere to Run – Love On The Run Series

In Plain Sight – Covert Justice Series

Saving Agent Tanner – Covert Justice Series

Every Beat – Covert Justice Series

Framed For Murder – A Scorpion Team Series Coming soon from Love Inspired Suspense

Deadly Memories – A Scorpion Team Series from Love Inspired Suspense

Rocky Mountain Pursuit - A Scorpion Team Series from Love Inspired Suspense

Forgotten Past – From Love Inspired Suspense

Rescue Me – A Second Chance, Montana Romance

Marry Me – A Second Chance, Montana Romance

Dear Me – A Second Chance, Montana Romance

Love Me Tender – A Second Chance, Montana Romance

A Family For Christmas – Treasure Of The Rockies Series

The Prodigal's Redemption – Treasure Of The Rockies Series

Montana Skies - Treasure Of The Rockies Series

Made in the USA
Las Vegas, NV
02 December 2022